Azura's Journey through the
Enchanted Forest

Story by: Mckayla Julian

Illustrations by Magnus Weinhauser

ISBN: 978-1-998243-48-8

Ahelia Publishing, LLC
Box 532 Augusta, MT 59410
aheliapublishing@outlook.com

www.aheliapublishing.org

Published in the USA
Printed in the USA

This book is dedicated to our beloved Great-Grandma, Grandma, Mom, Aunt, Sister, and friend, Geraldine May Anderson. Your words of wisdom, heart of gold, and philanthropic spirit proudly live on through us and the work we continue to do here in honor of you.

Not so long ago, in a cozy, enchanted forest, lived a young owl named Azura.

Azura was known for her bright green eyes and her love for stargazing.

But, one particular day, some dark clouds appeared in her heart, and she began to feel sad and alone.

She didn't understand why.

One evening, as Azura took a flight through her favorite enchanted forest, her friend Cash, the squirrel, noticed her sad eyes.

He asked, "Azura, are you okay?"

Azura blinked away a tear and replied, "I'm not sure. I've felt very sad and lonely lately, even when the stars are out."

Cash smiled kindly.

"Azura, it's okay to feel this way sometimes. We all have stormy days in our hearts. You're not alone, and I'm here for you."

Cash invited Azura to visit a wise old turtle named Geri, who lived by the shimmering pond.

Geri had seen many seasons and understood the ups and downs of life.

Azura wasn't sure if it would help, but decided to try it.

Geri listened carefully to Azura's feelings.

She explained, "Your heart, like the sky, can have storms and feel big feelings. What's important is to remember that there are friends, family, and wise old turtles like me who can help you find the sunshine again."

Azura felt a bit lighter after talking to Geri and sharing her feelings with Cash. She realized that it was okay to ask for help and that she wasn't alone in her journey.

As the days went by, Azura started to feel a little better. She continued to stargaze and, with Cash's help, learned to dance in the rain when the clouds gathered in her heart.

They played games and shared stories, brightening the dark days.

One day, Azura saw another friend, Bruin the bear, looking sad by the river. Azura remembered what she had learned and went over to Bruin.

"Bruin, are you okay?" she asked.

Bruin sniffled and said, "No. I'm not. I've been feeling lonely, too."

Azura patted Bruin on the arm and said, "You're not alone, and it's okay to ask for help.

Let's visit Geri together."

With Geri's guidance and their friendship, Azura, Cash, and Bruin learned to face their stormy days.

They realized that reaching out to friends and wise old turtles was a sign of strength, not weakness.

The forest became a place of support and understanding, where every creature knew they could share their stormy skies and find help from friends who cared.

They learned that they could get through any storm together and find the sunshine again.

Milton Keynes UK
Ingram Content Group UK Ltd.
UKHW051536310324
440283UK00010BA/45